Undone

Undone

Poems by Kim Bridgford

David Robert Books

Published by David Robert Books
P.O. Box 541106
Cincinnati, OH 45254-1106

ISBN: 0-9717371-4-2
LCCN: 2002117099

Poetry Editor: Kevin Walzer
Business Editor: Lori Jareo

Typeset in Iowan Old Style by WordTech Communications,
Cincinnati, OH

Visit us on the web at www.davidrobertbooks.com

Cover Art: Jo Yarrington, Tikkun Olam series (Aldrich Museum),
© 2000

Cover Layout: M. Scott Douglass

Acknowledgments

Acumen: "The Boy Who Cried Wolf," "The Memory Stone"

The Chariton Review: "Ash," "Free Fall," "The Leaves," "Looking Back," "What the Trees Know"

The Christian Science Monitor: "Emily Dickinson"

Connecticut Review: "Beneath the Shabbiness," "The Drowning," "Eighteen," "In the Leaves"

The Formalist: "Evening"

The Iowa Review: "The Argument"

Literature and Belief: "Mercy," "Rapture"

The Malahat Review: "The Cancer Sonnets"

North American Review: "The Suicide"

Poetry Nottingham International: "Someone Is Out There"

Poetrybay: "All That Glitters Is Not Gold"

Rattapallax: "The Reckoning"

South Carolina Review: "Ars Poetica"

Southern Humanities Review: "The Fight"

Thumbscrew: "Living in the World"

Wascana Review: "In the Trees"

Willow Review: "In the Woods"

Writers' Forum: "The Blessing"

I am grateful to my teacher, Donald Justice, whose impact on my life and work has been immeasurable and lasting. I would also like to thank the National Endowment for the Arts and Fairfield University for their generous support. Finally, I owe a debt of gratitude to Kevin Walzer and Lori Jareo for believing in my project.

For Pete and Nick

Contents

II.

III.

IV.

I.

Love Leaves the Sestina for Greener Pastures

The sestina eats Godiva chocolates in bed,
And then she weeps. Love's leaving her for poems
That have more variation, so he says,
As he pulls on his pants, zips his good-bye.
Well, hell with him. All that Victoria's Secret—
The black chemise, the complicated clothes—

Didn't do a thing. You're boring, clothes
Or no clothes, he told her. She clawed the bed
And wept, told him she'd fulfill his darkest secret,
But he was already elsewhere, with the poems
He'd left at first, with hardly a good-bye,
To be with Sestina. Now each time she says,

"Six," he wants to die, each time she says,
"Let's drink martinis and take off our clothes
To all our favorite high school songs." Good-bye
To all that. Perhaps Sonnet is in bed,
He hopes alone, although her passion for poems
Like her runs high, a sequence her darkest secret

Besides the chains. The villanelle's all secret,
Thinks she's nineteen. "Kiss me, Darling," she says
Through smoke-rings, reading in a whisper the poems
She's written herself. Villanelle sans clothes,
Her rhyme, her punctuation, is the bed
Itself: free verse the prelude to good-bye.

Love thinks of Couplets and the quick good-bye,
Ballad and her penchant for the secret
Found in *The National Enquirer.* Rondeau in bed
With Concrete Poem, so the lead story says,
Then murder! Words in circles: in the clothes,
The bed sheets, all the clippings of found poems

The evidence. He should give up on poems,
Try some fiction, but then he'd say good-bye
To romance, whose formal trappings are the clothes
Of poetry. A poem is like a secret
In the dark; prose is "he says, she says,"
Then the stripping of all sex-play from the bed.

Better the poems, the charm of each good-bye.
Each memory of the bed is like a secret
That says, "Here, Love," then reaches for the clothes.

Poetry Cheese

A poet's hope: to be
like some valley cheese,
local, but prized everywhere.
—W.H. Auden

People should want their poetry like cheese—
On pizzas, on their sandwiches, with wine.
In supermarkets, you can make the case

For poetry: the villanelles, like bries,
For parties; long free verse to eat alone.
People should want their poetry like cheese.

Like Velveeta, poetry will squeeze
Its feelings, in a burst, on a saltine.
In supermarkets, you can make the case.

Creative writers, English Ph.Ds
Will package poems, like farmers from Wisconsin.
People should want their poetry like cheese.

Finally, there'll be a need to advertise.
Readings will appear on television.
In supermarkets, you can make the case:

More slim volumes! More anthologies!
Some well-made chapbooks for the impulse line.
People should want their poetry like cheese.
In supermarkets, you can make the case.

For Vanna White

You know what every poet does. The letters
Fall from your fingers as you unclothe phrases
One by one. You smile. Your hand eases
Meaning from nothing, while Pat Sajak flatters
The guests. How magical words are to us
Suddenly. Someone has bought a vowel.
Now the studio audience is full
Of poets, working through the omnibus
Of words and hoping for the perfect fit;
And, Vanna, you are there when the last click
Happens, when the letter comes through the thick
Tangle of communal guesswork into what
Can only be rightness, can only be
Your fingers on the pulse of poetry.

The Shoes of Imelda Marcos

Okay. There were too many of them, and yet
There was a fascination with the way
A fetish could explode into decay.
We wondered at mathematics of the feet
And came up gasping. Sneakers, flats, low heels:
What was there to wear that merited
These rows the Philippines inherited?
It was the genius of the espadrilles
That took our eyes from what they should have seen:
The rows of nothingness that stood in place
Of what a culture could have bought. Entice
The world with goods, and we will stand in line,
Forgetting in the glitter of an hour
The people that were walked on for that power.

All That Glitters Is Not Gold

Sleep with an idol. Here's what happens then:
There's glitter on your face, and hair, and mouth.
You like it, make the coffee as you glisten.

At first the glitter covers up the human:
A drinking problem. Cigarettes. False teeth.
Sleep with an idol. Here's what happens then:

One day you find his failure on your skin.
It's wet like paint, transparent as a moth.
You hate it, make the coffee as you glisten.

What happened to the glamor of the pen?
What happened to the voice? It wasn't truth.
Sleep with an idol. Here's what happens then.

You know he doesn't want to be alone,
That words mean nothing to him next to youth.
You hate it, make the coffee as you glisten.

You call your first an adolescent passion;
You keep your next one shiny with a cloth.
Sleep with an idol. Here's what happens then:
You like it, make the coffee as you glisten.

The Wizard of Oz

It's the story of our longing, Kansas
To Oz, immediate friendships on the road,
The evil recognizable that haunts us.
Want a brain? It's yours. Whatever the need,
You take the path laid out in yellow bricks;
And if the end turns out to be a sham,
Confront it, and there's something you can fix.
O Dorothy, sick of your life and wanting home,
Adventuress with Toto at your side,
Who wouldn't want a chance to take a walk
With ruby slippers? Some might find it odd,
Your first refusal of the shoes, might mock
Your act as strangely disingenuous,
When everything you did you did for us.

Georgia O'Keeffe

The flowers are so huge, they make her think
Of death or sex: something to swallow up
What life is. What would it be like, the stink
Of such a flower in her hair: a tilted cup,
A bathtub, a bed? Sometimes another's dream
Can be stripped and made more commonplace.
Untie the fear, and the isolated scream
Is simply odd; the O-gape on the face
Is to be studied. Enter, then, the weed
Or burr. An object held so close is now
Miraculous, strangely exotic, odd.
The trick is the minutiae of how:
The curtain wafting like a sail, the sun
Convulsing, the body off its track, undone.

Ars Poetica

For Georgia O'Keeffe

You are stern, and yet your flowers are not:
Voluptuous as whores, their petticoats
The interior of the body. To touch these throats
Is knowing what to keep and what to forfeit.

At dawn, the paintings wonder at their sex,
And lie like lovers in the after-art
(Their minds reliving what transpired in part),
Heavy in the arms of paradox.

The Suicide

When the suicide moved in across the street,
People knew her as the woman with blonde hair.
She hadn't decided on her method yet:

A gun? Some pills? The blood released from its knot
Of life? At first, there was nothing to fear
When the suicide moved in across the street.

She couldn't sleep at all, she said. At night
She wove her drunken mind around a star.
She hadn't decided on her method yet.

Later, they read the signs: the way each thought
Stumbled on the grass, the telling whisper.
When the suicide moved in across the street,

She tried to tell them how immediate
Death was, how soft, its under-wings like Mother.
She hadn't decided on her method yet.

They didn't hear. She asked for tea, the gate
Closing in her eyes. She asked for sugar.
When the suicide moved in across the street,
She hadn't decided on her method yet.

Anne Sexton

In all the pictures you are smiling, sexy,
Beautiful. You seduced the audience,
Trembling as you offered up your demons.

Striptease. Soultease. Naked in your poetry,
You lay there, quiet, sucking on your death;
Then something called you back: the blood and music
Of your art. The wandering poet of the sick,
You stood at podiums and howled the truth.

No audience on the last day. Alone,
Wrapped in your mother's coat, the music on,
You said good-bye to everything you knew.
You who gave yourself to love, to sun,
To writing, you who were brilliant and insane,
Made all the words line up and mourn for you.

Emily Dickinson

I think about the days she sewed her poems
With threads of ink that held the sounds between
The words. She put her heart down in her rhymes
And understood that somewhere in the skin
There is an answer for each line, a chorus
That she traced within herself. Why pause
Right there? a student asks as if to stress
The point. The answer is in earthly laws
Of conversation, how to frame them so
The texture of the momentary speech
Lasts. Think of your memory as a ragged row
Of utterances that you would like to reach
For when you wished. Impossible. She chose
To try: with words—then dashes—between those.

The Importance of Words

The problem with King Lear was not his pride.
Beloved, when we wake, let us both laugh.
He wanted something more before he died.

You didn't know that age transforms to need,
That words make up the wheat as well as chaff.
The problem with King Lear was not his pride.

Our poems, bequeathed from beauty and from blood,
Will show how we held wisdom by the scruff.
He wanted something more before he died.

A candle is beautiful, as is the toad,
And the plainest conversation of your sleeve.
The problem with King Lear was not his pride.

The dew, without a voice, must still be read,
The sunlight on the grass, the falling leaf.
He wanted something more before he died.

I'm wrong to think that speaking shapes the deed,
And yet how else could I endure your love?
The problem with King Lear was not his pride.
He wanted something more before he died.

Someone Is Out There

Someone is trying to say something now.
It's quiet. Listen. The sound is like a cry.
Or worse: the rusty low calls from below,
Like a palimpsest of mockery.

It's quiet. Listen. The sound is like a cry.
Crows are like that, their cacophonous ash
Like a palimpsest of mockery
On the lawn. You listen for the hook to catch.

Crows are like that, their cacophonous ash
All *caw, caw,* and moan. You get caught in the sound.
On the lawn, you listen for the hook to catch.
The air gets darker, and the shadows blend.

All *caw, caw,* and moan—you get caught in the sound.
Is your neighbor dying? The children in bed?
The air gets darker, and the shadows blend.
Will there be some catastrophe instead?

Is your neighbor dying? The children in bed?
You listen to the chipping at your soul
(Will there be some catastrophe instead?)
As your mind wraps around each syllable.

You listen to the chipping at your soul
Or worse: the scratchy low sounds from below.
As your mind wraps around each syllable,
Someone is trying to say something now.

Sonnet for a Sick Child

He coughs. He coughs again. We're all awake,
The three of us. He climbs into our bed
And coughs, then falls asleep. Our eyeballs ache
With the dust of nights spent just like this, his head
Beneath the crevice of an arm. I dream
Of sleep the way I used to dream of sex:
Romantic possibility.
                 Now time
To start the day, and still his small white socks
Kick my leg in sleep. He coughs. And yet
Whatever needs to be done, I rush to do.
His pajama top has a jet plane on it,
And says, "Let's fly away." Smiling, I go
To get his juice, but he is drowsing off.
If I lie down beside him, then he'll cough.

Living in the World

My son has taught me how to live in the world.
Dogs, dead worms, the healing power of bandaids
Are enough to make the day worthwhile. He reads
Now, and a sign, like "CAUTION" or "DANGER," will yield
Itself up to him, glowing like God's Word.
He shouts the message out in capitals.
How magical each day is, like the carrels
At the library, festooned with a shining sword
For summer reading. *Come over here, Mom,*
He says, and we play tea party for a while,
Then pretend we're going on the train.
We close our eyes. There's a rising of the steam,
And soon our faces shine with wet soot. Rule
Number one is anything can happen.

Profiles

The day our teacher drew a silhouette
Of each of us, and put our profiles up,
We tried to guess whose cut-out head was what,
But didn't realize we'd need a map.

With a finger, Teacher showed us what she drew.
It fascinated us, that sideways line;
Yet we had trouble following each clue:
The differences in profile barely seen.

But when our mothers came how soon they saw
The eyelash curls of one, the family jaw,
The forehead speaking of the father's side.
Somehow we knew our mothers understood
The smell behind our ear, our body's shape
Like fingerprints they carried in their sleep.

What the Trees Know

Perhaps the trees are leaning there in grief,
A strangled cry between their leafy hands.
Perhaps the wind has shaken their belief.

Or maybe ours. A gravestone's bas-relief
Mocks angels petrified by circumstance.
Perhaps the trees are leaning there in grief

To ponder this: Time is just a common thief
Of loose ends. They pucker into absence.
Perhaps the wind has shaken our belief,

Followed by the trembling underneath,
Like a tune the body knows in ignorance.
Perhaps the trees are leaning there in grief.

Whatever life has carved is only brief:
The tease of art, our last inheritance.
Perhaps the wind has shaken our belief.

Kisses mark us in a momentary wreath,
Like passionate shadows of extravagance.
Perhaps the trees are leaning there in grief.
Perhaps the wind has shaken their belief.

Little Red Riding Hood Grows Up

Sometimes she feels the wolves behind her eyes,
The stealthy ease

Of their shadows and their breath. Everything's dark,
Even the work

Of love. When you've been eaten and released,
That is the cost.

Like a statue in the thick of what's grown wild,
She feels the old

Cry of fear along her bones. Who can
Forget what's in

The heart? The past is always merciless,
The same red dress,

The same door swinging open. A wolf's disguise
Reveals the ease

With which a single innocence can die.
Eternity

Is the moment before what is devoured,
Or what is shared.

Sometimes the birds can settle on her hair.
She doesn't scare.

Childhood Love

he no longer had any of his childhood love for her
—Ursula Hegi

Like sticky sweets that you no longer want,
This childhood love. The lap, the cake, the breasts,
The one-more hug. How easy to refuse the crusts
From one whose need was never what you meant.

The hunger in her eyes, breath in your ear
Are different now, the words that whisper, *Wait.*
Yet it's the cloying fingertips, once light
On satin wrists, that make you languish for

Anything but these rooms of bric-a-brac.
Come home, the voice says, sugared from the past;
And while you want to go, there is a voice
That tells you what will happen when you're back:
The kiss on the lips, the death-smell of the lost,
The touch me there, my pretty boy. That's nice.

In the Leaves

After all your relatives have died,
There is nothing but the ache of dread,

Or worse: a savage emptiness around
The mutterings that you mistake for sound.

But they're just you—and what your mind believes
Is sorrow wrapped in sequences of leaves,

Like silver drifts of form. You find the past—
What never happened and what doesn't last—

Is like that. You don't know what happens now,
The calendar unthinkable as snow.

But at dawn, startled, you awake to pain
As if your family were dancing on a pin,

Your lashes full of tears. Who would know why
You're the one this side of eternity?

Every evening you are like the air:
Whispers of invisible despair.

Beneath the Shabbiness

Beneath the shabbiness of all your days
You find some moments strewn like wildest need
Grown quiet. Their secret comes with their surprise:
A finger-width of dream has sprung to seed.

Stop there. Push the pleasure of the greed:
The shine of spangles and the long applause
From years ago. Your wandering soul is laid
Beneath the shabbiness of all your days.

Yet memory is fickle. A baby cries,
And then is gone. The day your daughter died,
Your arms felt limp as lost parentheses.
You find some moments strewn like wildest need.

It's easier not to want too much: the odd
Markings of a leaf; the way a shutter sighs
As if to say, "Come back"; a teapot's load
Grown quiet. Their secret comes with their surprise.

You wish the world was not made up of eyes
That judge the dingy surfaces. Instead
Look: underneath this faded enterprise
A finger-width of dream has sprung to seed.

Perhaps that's how the human life is made:
To keep that hope, like shining in disguise,
When time says no. To live is to recede
Until what you loved most of all is a tease
        Beneath the shabbiness.

Mercy

Mercy is a custard pie, the slip
Of a teardrop,

And then the free fall into the new air
That is your fear.

It's true. The problem with mercy is that honey
Never gave any

Clear answers to anybody, thus the sweet
And sour, the fate

Of Jesus Christ. Why is there nausea for
Each redeemer,

The snake in the heart? Why is each kindness weak
With a soul-ache?

Force is plain. Better the pitchfork, the thin
Belt landing on

Small legs; oh, better to sleep without bread.
Love doesn't add

Up, and for this we need what's merciful,
Christ when he fell.

Rapture

Sex and religion claim it: the deep swoon
That shoves reason

Aside. How else explain loss? For in shrill
Heart-thrummings still

In memory comes our deepest longing. Why
Else would there be

Babies in anonymous earth, or scraps
Of saints in heaps

For sale? Transcendence is the way to God
And through our load:

Flickerings of the sharpest joy that we know now
By passing through.

The Boy Who Cried Wolf

How can he tell them that he sees wolf-shapes
Even in their eyes? Each time he starts
To speak, he watches what happens in the gaps:
The tightening of the mouth, the eye-slits
Of disappointment. They have had enough.
But if they saw the swirling secrets of
That fur, the pack, like horror underneath,
Wouldn't they speak too? He has no love
Of this life, only faith: that when they come
For him, one day, someone will save his name,
Telling of a boy who knew the terrors
Of life so well he saw no other thing
And so could only bleat to death his warning
Of a wolf. Meanwhile they pointed out his errors.

Blind-Man's Bluff

The beauty of the earth is not enough,
The preachers say, caressing heaven's sleeve.
The mortal is a game of blind-man's bluff.

The scientists are looking for the proof
In facts and not romantic make-believe.
The beauty of the earth is not enough.

The businessmen are gilded and aloof,
Reminding presidents they are naive.
The mortal is a game of blind-man's bluff.

The poor wait in line, shuffling for food-stuff,
Tired of do-gooders' recitative.
The beauty of the earth is not enough.

The sensual prefer a powder-puff,
And wine: a crash of noise on New Year's Eve.
The mortal is a game of blind-man's bluff.

Can we, in love, take living by the scruff,
Or does the world know only how to grieve?
The beauty of the earth is not enough.
The mortal is a game of blind-man's bluff.

Evening

On evenings when the light is hard to catch
And trees are deepening shadows on the dark,
When souls are indecisive as a match,
And fireflies leave a temporary mark,
I think of you. Perhaps it's just the way
The dying colors emphasize the loss
Of time, or maybe twilight's disarray
Reminds me of your tendency to gloss
Our feelings into something else: a blur
Of anger softened into pain. It's there
I want to stop, but, like the smallest spur
Of splendor, hearts can't stop in moments rare
As this. They take the course of dissonance
That scatters through a love's ambivalence.

The Reckoning

To see the beautiful in everything,
You must be schooled in nuances of loss;
You must be ready for the reckoning.

The blues are palette for the evening,
Reminder of the depth of human cost
To see the beautiful in everything.

Women, with children scooped from suffering,
Remember the fulfillment of the cross:
You must be ready for the reckoning.

The broken vow, the slow extinguishing
Of love—it is impossible for most
To see the beautiful in everything.

The aged, wrinkled from their wandering,
Are restless for the shadowed way across.
You must be ready for the reckoning.

The earth is cracked with ancient clamoring,
And fallen fragrances are stiff with frost.
To see the beautiful in everything,
You must be ready for the reckoning.

The Blessing

The other day I wondered what you meant.
You said that death was something you knew well—
That you had blessed it, given it consent.

Instead, I raged at the incompetent,
The only way I had to master hell:
To counteract the words I thought you meant.

You didn't offer me admonishment.
Not you. You called it pointless to rebel—
The trick was blessing it, giving it consent,

Then dismissing it as irrelevant.
Your face was calm. *I learned to cast a love-spell
On each moment.* I wondered what you meant,

Then saw the nature of your argument:
Forget it. Only God was immortal,
And He had blessed it, given it consent.

In death, how could you be so eloquent?
In love, mon frere, you have no parallel.
The other day I cried at what you meant—
That you had blessed me, given me consent.

Eighteen

The year that sorrow took me by the cuff,
I didn't know it by that name. I was
Eighteen and thought that living was enough
For anybody. Sylvia Plath, whose
Pain recommended putting what was felt
First, understood. With loneliness as deep
And pure as death, I practiced being svelte
And gagged, while friends who needed beauty-sleep
Refused to talk. And this was what it meant
To grow up, I thought. To separate. To
Betray. I gained weight in discouragement,
Met Aristotle, Sartre, then was through
With that year. Awful. Painful nausea.
And that was what I knew of Sylvia.

The Fight

She said that hatred had nothing to do
With it, and you said, no, she was mistaken;
The words went on like that, with just the two
Of you in a space of despair. You used to awaken
In arms so tangled with love that you would laugh,
One person! Only one! the way a charm
Works: the great boots of evil stomping off
Into the clouds. Imagine now when harm
Wins out: the witch refashioning the routes
Of guilty pleasure, made easy for climbing
By desire. *Now, come*; and you do with doubts
In knots beneath your hands. Who knows the clamoring
Of your heart? Rapunzel no longer lives in the skies,
And a stumble on stones takes out your eyes.

The Drowning

You told me of the other life you'd led:
The woman pausing in the after-glare
Of kisses—his on whose?—and love thread-bare
With lies. Your mouth was dusty then, you said;
The earth was flat with death. And garlanded
Like Ophelia you went down: everywhere
Choking bewilderment, a thoroughfare
Of fishes.
       Later they attributed
Your act to illness, and you didn't say
That trust was like a flaking in your heart
And water love's most useful metaphor.
You blinked. He left. And it wasn't doomsday.
You learned that much: and yet there is an art,
You found, in learning how to underscore.

Ash

She pictures imaginary letters sent
From places she won't go, exquisite flags
Of his remorse from every continent

On earth. He's gone. But when he packed his bags
It wasn't real, the way some lovers' quarrels
Become wild terror swirling on the crags

That drop to death. Footsteps in old hotels
Echo what's lost to surfaces, the hum
Of elevators speaking clumsy farewells

Between floors. Each night she can picture him
Opening a room: the lamplight and the bed
The passage out of ordinary time,

Along with a picture inexpertly painted,
Flowers in a vase, or figures drawn out of
All proportion with the earth. He said

He missed the world. That's when the shriveled wreath
Was laid, like a vagrant's gathering of sticks,
Upon her chest. Since then he has been off

Wandering cities, stepping into wrecks
Of giant stone. He always liked the way
That history was delivered from the texts

Without words, the millennial entry
Of men whose names became erased in granite;
Or far-flung space sent down by destiny

Or chance. She puts her faith in intimate
Details: a drawing or a poem, a rock
More for the person than the place, the weight

Of shared time. One day they began to talk,
She wanting home, and he a hemisphere
With room. Tonight she feels it helps to walk,

The shadows of the twilight like a lure
Of broken beauty, the pull of what's at stake
Before the dark. The merest light can never

Last. She knows this, understands the ache,
And takes the drifting streets, each offering
A jump rope song, a laugh, the bric-a-brac

Of ordinary life. The littering
Of lawns by petals, thick as fragrant snow,
Catches her up, keeps her from remembering

Absence, so full are they, but, like the slow
Scattering of love, they lose their sense
Of what they are and where they want to go:

The dying stems the shreds of eloquence.
She stops. Now everyone is going in:
To love and laugh, to sleep, just experience

A life. So much to let go of. How thin
It is to be alone. Even her hands
Seem ghostly, almost as if her skeleton

Were breaking through its momentary bonds
To grasp the ashy nothing of what ends.

In the Woods

Remember how the woods were dark with grief?
The brambles held you back; you lost your way.
Your heart fell down as common as a leaf,
Its brilliance caught, and squandered, in decay.

The brambles held you back; you lost your way
In a shadow. Cool it was, and familiar,
Its brilliance caught, and squandered, in decay,
Telling of what is lost and what is true

In a shadow. Cool it was, and familiar
Like childhood warnings or the absent, slow
Telling of what is lost and what is true.
That night you waited for all your love to go.

Like childhood warnings or the absent, slow
Splashes of a boat, death came and then it went.
That night you waited for all your love to go.
And then you wondered what such passing meant.

Nothing? Adrift there in the dooms of space?
Your heart fell down as common as a leaf.
When you thought of how you'd never see his face,
Remember how the woods were dark with grief?

In the Trees

In the shiver of a winter's air,
The trees question the wind and snow. They move
In the almost night and sing. Now I can hear
What's melancholy about the world, when love
Is stripped to this. It's like the hissing kettle
On the stove, or the snake that spelled it out
Through tainted bites of loss. Their voices curdle
In darkness, and the serenade of late
Desire chills me. Is there always the kiss
Of fear, like a branch that scrapes against the house,
And sounds like something lost? I tell you this,
Whoever you are, because in the merest trace
Of movement, I see myself and also you:
Occasions for the wind to travel through.

The Leaves

Along the ashy avenues of fall
She hears a whispering, as if the leaves
Are telling what they know: part miracle,

Part hopelessness, like mutterings from graves
When nothing but the wind reads out the names
From chiselled lips of loss. She loved the thieves

Of summer all her life—the muted dreams
Made rich to store the pumpkins in, the air
Half apples and half snow, the harvest themes

Of fullness. Why did moments not come clear—
The ones the elders spoke of from their bones
In wooden chairs? It was spectacular,

They said and meant both life and past, in tones
That read the dying of an evening's light
As truth. When she takes walks, she finds routines

Heartbreaking now—a child up reading late,
Her face transfixed by worried words, the scream
Of play by boys whose rules exaggerate

What it means to be men. The momentary gleam
Of supper tables rounds days out with prayers,
And the children bow their pretty heads. A slam

Of a door flings anger out and in, while stairs
Show lovers caught in kisses meant to last
All night. She knows, when she looks at the stars,

That they're the closest thing that she can trust
Forever. The leaves surrender in a rush,
And all their utter loveliness is lost

Too soon. She never listened very much,
But maybe that's what comes with age—to know
And then to die. She stops at the furthest reach

Of leaves, looks down the tunneled avenue,
And sighs, then takes her footsteps lightly back
Through colors of a moment's last tattoo.

At the other end a boy and father rake
What's covered up their yard, in careful piles:
The filter on their lawn throughout the week.

The woman watches while the boy appeals
To something—father or the air—and flings
His body, like it's nothing, in the hills

Of leaves. He's buried there, but yet he sings
Of all that's lost and gained in broken things.

The Memory Stone

History does not mark the personal,
And yet, for most, that makes up life. Where is
The monument to love? No park is full
Of statues to it; the daily sacrifice
Of partners—sitting by sick-beds, grave stones,
Minds broken up by time—does not have weight
With records broken, wars based on who wins
And who does not. The momentary fate
Of a child fades with the news of who will lead
The country. Love, like nature, is transient—
The golden splendor of its leaf inlaid
With death. How can the proper sentiment
Be paid for dusk? Where is its memory stone?
Where is the passing moment that we own?

It Didn't Matter

It didn't matter, the way we thought it would:
The doll we couldn't have, and the hot tears
Clotted in sleep; the turtle we found dead
And buried, late, in whispers, under stars.

It didn't matter, the way we thought it would.
We fell, and other people laughed. We loved,
And other people turned our hearts to lead.
We lost our friends to accidents, and grieved.

It didn't matter, the way we thought it would:
The poems we thought would bring us sudden fame,
The way the days died quickly, like a seed,
The way it was easy to forget a name;

So why on our death-bed, when we let go
Does everything that didn't matter so?

Looking Back

Not once did we walk through that golden grass,
Miraculous

With promises we knew were to be kept,
Nor did we step

Through years with silver in their waves. No doubt
We wanted it.

How ordinary every day can be,
All history

Being chaos mixed with hope. The hour
Is just a lure.

That's the lesson of the old, the mind
Circling the end

With stories of toboggans on the ice,
The fateful choice

Of love around a ring. When tomorrow
Arrives, its blue

Is always momentary, always thick
With gnats, the tick

Of time. It never was that beautiful,
But each youthful

Memory is a frame to set our lives in gold,
A last foothold

On a passing life. When the lid goes down,
There is no one.

II.

The Argument

I.

I couldn't tell which one of us was wrong,
But what's the difference? Pride was between
Us, like the ice that's shaped from unforeseen
Weather, or like the recollected song
From another life. And who was headstrong?
Both. Who, with heart in hand, would intervene?
That's pride for you—unwilling to come clean,
And start again. I could speak of lifelong
Promises: like a lightning crown of leaves
That draws the eye in momentary gasps
Of brilliance, how the falling we love too,
That graceful drifting, like parentheses
Around the air, the lovely in collapse,
Surrender as the twilight rendezvous.

II.

Surrender as the twilight rendezvous
Of desire and desired: in short, your
Fulfillment—was that what the fight was for?
But what was coveted? You thought I knew,
And icy words kept preventing a true
Discussion. It was like a dark mirror
I struggled to make out, the interior
In shadows. You explained that you were through,
But with what? What did you want? Glittery things
Flashed in my mind, in heaps of falsity.
You never were that way. But maybe now
Was different. A baby's mutterings—
All sweetened vowels. But it couldn't be.
I couldn't have a baby anyhow.

III.

I couldn't have a baby anyhow,
But maybe you could. Maybe she was there
During the moments lust was everywhere
You looked, and when the notion of a vow
Seemed faint as buried words that won't allow
The reader passage, ruins of a prayer
Left for the scholars in the dust. In an air
Of incremental silence come somehow
From good—like any spoiling beauty, rust
In all the subtle crevices—I stood
With memories in hand, the days when all
Wherevers and wherefores were there with us,
And casual sounds of jazz and traffic would
Be counterpoint for love as usual.

IV.

Be counterpoint for love as usual;
Be salt to hand; be sugar to my lips;
Be water to most casual of sips;
Be data for the bibliographical;
Be mine. But no. Some preternatural
Force had become the twin of love, like whips
Inside our hearts, but ice, two frozen ships
Whose hulls scraped pieces of occasional
Touch. Anger never aided anyone,
And yet, like reinvented angry wheels,
We spun and spun. I wanted you to laugh,
But laughter needs to draw from unison—
The symphony a loving look reveals—
Not from the remnants of love's epitaph.

V.

Not from the remnants of love's epitaph,
But from its former wealth: was it too much,
This feast? I guess that paradise of touch
Like any other thing can go to chaff.
Yet constantly you scoffed at half and half —
Pure cream for you, fresh bread, and fruits with such
Unbearable undoing, like each clutch
And falling we had. In one photograph
Of you I love, you're biting off a peach,
The juice of miracle upon your chin.
You're six. You're sweet. You loved it even then:
The perishable passion in your reach.
Consider. Taste. The metaphor of sin.
The question tempting each of us was when.

VI.

The question tempting each of us was when:
When would you say? But on the other hand
I'd put the blame on you, your self-command,
When you might long to talk and think that men
Get placed in boxes—silent type again—
When it's just you. You tried to understand
A route with words, an inky, glutted land
Where language was the daily regimen,
The texture of existence filling the chink
Of despair. But for you it couldn't be.
How could those radiant phrases tip the scale,
When aching was inchoate, poised at the brink
Of nothing? With a lack of fluency,
We started making up with lovers' braille.

VII.

We started making up with lovers' braille,
The hieroglyphs of passion, the other route
We both could take. I closed my eyes to doubt
And, later, in your arms could hear each frail
Reminder of the world. With such detail—
The trees' languid treasure, with wind throughout
Its passing wealth, a laugh, a passing shout—
The ordinary life. Sloth? Ah. The scale
By which it all was judged. The after-time.
The stillness there. Exquisite hiding-place:
The kind the lonely search for in the long
Impressionable hours. It was sublime,
You said; I said that we were saving face.
I couldn't tell which one of us was wrong.

III.

The Cancer Sonnets

I.

How often does your heart feel sad like this?
How often do you wonder why you live?
Where's paradise? Where's metamorphosis?
Where's blossoming that knows how to forgive?
It's late. You're counting all the hours again;
You know that you should not. You know it's better
To lose yourself in anything as often
As your heart can tell you so. Perhaps the weather,
Unpredictable as the body's news,
Has something, has a daily miracle
Rich as the sky. Yet still the cancer blues
Play tunes upon your soul's harmonica.
How often have the dying fingered hope
Like something hidden in an envelope?

II.

How often does your heart feel sad like this?
You know that scholars, searching in the dust,
Want ruins to be whole, want memory's kiss
To kiss. They're just like you in that they must
Take brokenness, take random ignorance
And shape the news for others. Parchment calls
While cities burn and babies give up voice,
And students wait to hear it, the disciples
Of the word, while religion has archetypal lines
Like children's drawing books. You step in there
With colors of your own, but bold designs
Keep you from walking reckless out on air.
The story that starts in disobedience
Redeems itself in moments of transcendence.

III.

How often do you wonder why you live?
You never used to. Then you took each day
Like treasure and made dramatic narrative,
Moments spent like casual coins in play
You know now for the laughter. The circus
Camped on your front steps, where you read the palms
Of people searching for miraculous
Happenings told by a child. You sold love-charms,
Stones with healing power for the skin,
And fresh hope. Photographs show you in your dress
And bracelets, sign to show that you're within,
With money-box to show your seriousness.
When asked to conjure spirits from the dead,
You said you did such things up in your head.

IV.

Where's paradise? Where's metamorphosis?
Can it be here? Can it be just as close
As loving, just the ordinary bliss
Of touch? In bed, the casual arm across
The spent joy of another makes the time
On earth seem glorious, like a secret string
Unraveling inside. Poets call it rhyme.
What about the gardens, the murmuring
Of the earth? When the buds release their held
Beauty, like flags of small extravagance,
How can you think otherwise? When a child
Seizes the tunnel made by circumstance
And crowns such headlong travelling with birth,
There is a glimpse of paradise on earth.

V.

Where's blossoming that knows how to forgive?
How sad when time, so limited for you,
Makes you regret. You dwell on the negative,
Shrill phantoms of the past, the mind's tattoo
Of worst days: aching to apologize
Or replay moments when your weakest self
Faltered. Now you beg for playground compromise,
Not this battering, not the boy that knelt,
Weeping, from despair. A ball of scarlet shame
Uncurls in your throat. You drank too much
And passed out once without even the name
Of the man lying in your bed. Why touch
Such anguish now? Why bargain with a thief
That squanders your last moments like a leaf?

VI.

It's late. You're counting all the hours again.
Such madness strikes madness, like tired eyes
Seeing shapes. It's in the crevice in between
That you see life is a series of good-byes,
The friends who said they'd write and haven't yet,
The houses left behind, and the child you
Carried for six weeks, like an amulet
Bloody with questions. You find your strangest view
The vista back from childhood. Innocence
Was always dying, yet the pungent smell
Of knees scraped as they fell, the triggered sense
Of hopelessness, find you in a private hell
Where you want to whisper, *Pony bright!*
Your nonsense to make everything all right.

VII.

You know that you should not. You know it's better
To leave a world of playground dust behind
To dwell on more mature things: the first letter
Your father sent you and the last. His mind
Was finally at ease about you, a surprise
You fingered to shreds. Hadn't you done what
He wanted: won the ribbons—the first prize
For science in the second grade? And yet
He thought that you were lonely and you were.
You married shortly after. When he left
With someone blonde as gold, you said a prayer
About nothing, your numbness in that theft.
It's not the kind of thing you're proudest of,
To hold the public shards of private love.

VIII.

To lose yourself in anything as often
As pigeons wind their rounding gate toward home;
As easily as flowers in a coffin
Of earth rise from the dead, the shut, sweet loam
Whose promise, even after all the years,
Surprises with its fragrant voice. The nurse
Is coming back tomorrow; you hope your fears
Recoil like the fairy tale curse
That finds another victim. The morphine
Is the last stage to be played, which you know
The way a gambler knows a slot machine,
Just loss, loss, loss, or a possible row
Of sevens. But most step bankrupt into time
Made loose and dreary in the interim.

IX.

As your heart can tell you so, perhaps the weather
Is the easiest way to find your circumstance—
Not just made easier, but nature's offer
Betrays the human's promise not to dance
And makes the sickest fingers start to snap.
It's true you've thought of nature as a source,
But what of books? You know that roses drop
Their way to death, but words can reinforce
The sensual moment plucked from life. The ones
You've dared to make yourself into a poem
Have taken time, like yarn, in richest tones
And woven multicolored textures home.
You're worried cancer's words will tangle there
Into a gnarl of knots beside your chair.

X.

Unpredictable as the body's news:
Some weather; rain; the love of first-time love;
The tragic answers you take home as dues
Of your religion; babies taking off
Into the world, their steps a blurry strand
Toward anything but you, the creaking swing,
A moth, the sifting surfaces of sand,
The metaphor for nearly everything
On earth. Today you search for what can last,
And yet you find yourself bewildered by
Change, as if the blueprint of all loveliness
Were ruined in a moment. In mockery
Your life is gone. You think of the mirror's glass
Revealing the debacle of your face.

XI.

Has something, has a daily miracle
Convinced you not to die? It's up to you
They say, like stern tongues from an oracle,
In their white robes. It's hypocritical
Leaving life to the one whose lower back
Could wrack the world with pain. Tell them to take
Their own advice, but just as an attack
Can make you feel as if the whole heartache
Of God is with you, so you know that words
Spoken in the tone of anger leave the ear
Unmoved by argument, but hurting, like birds
Rained down upon. No point in being there;
No point in anything that hurts another;
No point in having hatred when it's over.

XII.

Rich as the sky, yet still the cancer blues
Have settled in your soul. So much for money.
So much for velvet draperies and pillows.
So much for America's milk and honey.
What's common is the journey through the soul:
The chaos of the dying days, the rites
You find yourself upholding. It's the fool
Who lives in ignorance, as if the fights
Of the flesh are enough. You know they never are.
You must bow down to being and must know
The dance of humankind is never far
From thinking out the shape of final tableau.
What's it all meant? What does the present mean?
These questions shape the monotony between.

XIII.

Play tunes upon your soul's harmonica.
Have someone bathe you, then comb out your hair,
As if the counting mattered. Erotica
Is fine, but mostly truth is found in where
The gesture meets the knowing, whether nurse
Does this or friend. You deserve the grace of touch:
Coffee in a special cup, a favorite verse
Written so that the tears come soon and overmuch.
Oh, blessed woman, think of heavy cream,
The smell of soup, the taste of Stilton cheese,
Crackers and wine, the call of *carpe diem*
That takes the moment for its taste of ease.
It's plenty, living out remaining days,
As if the world were chocolate tossaways.

XIV.

How often have the dying fingered hope,
Like something solid beneath Jesus' sleeve?
How often have they washed their souls in soap
To get some mercy? Those who can believe
Are peaceful at the end, but since the last
We see is just the tissue, just the mesh
Between the now and then, we hold too fast
And long to only what we know: the flesh
Weakened by age or illness. It is all
We have to spend our loving gestures on:
What's here, shaped as the mortal push and pull
Between the flesh and soul, a sweet onion
We peel if we can stand the sudden tears
That represent the spiral of the years.

XV.

Like something hidden in an envelope:
The next to this, the blessing here beside
The earth itself or where? Now we must grope
Our mortal way, on a rainy hillside
That in a step of wonder turns to sun.
The metaphors aren't lost on us, the first
To think our stumble to oblivion.
There at your window you see the first burst
Of light, and what has that light ever meant
But light? Today will bring the morphine, then
The slow surrender, the abandonment
Of all that's caused you grief. You are pleased when
You know how little pain is left to bear,
Swallowed in the nonsense of the air.

IV.

Free Fall

I.

The leaves are bright as kisses on the air,
Then fall to death. Love is like that, she thinks,
Who sees in the perilous free fall a surrender
She's lived with all her life. Still, she gives thanks
For what she has: her health, a view of sky
That puts both hell and heaven on display.
Some nights she feels the mutability
Of her own skin, the tracing of decay,
But framed in spectacular fireworks of breath.
She sees smoke drift in subtle messages,
Then turns to see some children practice death
Like masters. They dramatize the passages
In ways that capture the hyperbolic yearning
Of the soul in the last felt moment of its burning.

II.

Those fearless deaths in wayward piles of leaves
Remind her of the moments in her life
That gleam like careless jewels, the kind she sieves
Her memories for. How untold human grief
Gives birth to love and days of happiness
Is a mystery. One day she woke,
And the light dropped shadows on her nakedness;
And her eyes were full of what she couldn't speak.
Once, in a car, she felt the world like a print
From her fingers, only something she could have
Made, her husband talking, her son asquint
In the light, a day she'd pocket and then save
For later. In the moment's souvenir
The leaves are bright as kisses on the air.

III.

One boy springs up—the leaves a mask he's made,
A monster of the autumn. Then he laughs.
He's already learned the mix of shade
And light, the way that *almosts* and *what ifs*
Can change a life. It makes the woman pause
At her own: the time her car swerved from disaster,
The lumps that surfaced in her breast, the freeze
Of terror at the footsteps moving faster
In the dark. She has survived all this like the boy—
This peek-a-boo of terror—whose lost friends
Surface from the piles of leaves to bury
Him alive. There's a chase that briefly transcends
Time. Laughing, they tumble like tiddlywinks,
Then fall to death. Love is like that, she thinks.

IV.

To live alone is to know the footpaths of the soul,
To have the time to sit and think, and then to wander
Over the past. There time itself is malleable,
Just as all the elders said: the lost splendor
Of childhood found through a moment's noose.
Other days, the heft of a memory might
Surprise with its temporary lease,
And the feeling of this melancholy surfeit
Catches in the throat. If her husband hadn't left,
Would she have understood her self so well?
Now she knows the necessary craft
Of growing old, the paradoxical
Gift of loss. Time goes to the wanderer
Who sees in the perilous free fall a surrender.

V.

The children are playing tag now, for a while
Leaving leaves alone. She watches them
As the sky turns. It takes so much to feel
Anymore, and then so little, like a hymn
Whose words are ordinary, then the tears
Along the heart. From the majesty of dusk
To the pompom on a child's hat, she stirs
Her offerings and understands the task
Of being human is impossible.
How to do it all at once and be
In proper balance? The cup struggles to be full,
Then something else drains it all away.
The result is the constant source of angst
She's lived with all her life. Still she gives thanks.

VI.

Someone has a flashlight; he winks in and out,
Like a firefly, with echoes of surprise at just
What light can do. Then someone gives a shout,
And it's dinnertime. A few stay back to joust
With sticks. The woman makes a cup of tea,
Then returns to see them outlined there
In beautiful violence. Eternity
Passes as they pretend to be that rare
Combination—man and child—for whom
Danger is an art that comes from a game.
The woman wonders what they're like at home—
If each lost mother gathers her son when the dream
Is over, and, by the door, lets out a sigh
For what she has: her health, a view of sky.

VII.

The night is hardest for her. Next she goes
For a walk. She's startled by what she sees there
As if, to a momentary God, the rows
Of lives have offered themselves in a clear
Vision. So much for inwardness, the cupped
Future in a fortuneteller's hands. Now all
Choices can be hers: the boy enwrapt
With Proust, the girl in black who'll never tell
Her mother she's in love. It's obvious:
The kisses she wears like scars, food she sees
As time that's wasted. An old man, cut loose
From life, rocks forward to sublimities.
Sometimes there's art: the far-flung mastery
That puts both hell and heaven on display.

VIII.

She wonders if she had been someone else
If she'd been happier, or greater, queen
Of something she can't name, if all the false
Starts have happened because she's been between
What's been and should have been. If she could tell
The girl who suffers out of love that he
Will leave her, what would change? Each miracle
Comes from choice, placed within a destiny.
The chains of consequence coil into the dark,
Eden's metaphor. Meanwhile the harsh
Wail of an ambulance will take the arc
Of thought and drive it elsewhere, with her wish
No one dies, then: *It isn't me, it isn't me.*
Some nights she feels the mutability.

IX.

When she moves past the houses to the choirs
Of trees with tossled bits of talk above
The avenues, she's in a world that soars
With every light and shadow, a leafy nave
That makes her worshipful that she has silence.
This delicacy reminds her of how time
Has changed her, how the patina of reverence
Illuminates her mapwork like a rhyme
With God. Some days when she looks at her stunned
Face in the mirror, she watches the bones
Beneath, which shape the sorrow of her end.
The trees all whisper with their dying suns
To remember the beautiful calligraphy
Of her own skin, the tracing of decay.

X.

On her way home, she thinks of how the earth
Has always called her, how the simplest snow
Can fill her with a calm like church. The worth
Of this or that flat stone flung in adieu
Cannot be weighed, except in touch or sight.
Sometimes she's felt her pain explode at a V
Of birds in a sweep of instinctual birthright
Or the flowers lifting their Easter heads for free
Out of snow. When Christ walked on the water,
She's thought of his feet, their solitary grace
Holding him aloft. That is what he taught her
About life, seizing each wonder from a place
And making it a home, an eternal truth
But framed in spectacular fireworks of breath.

XI.

In bed, she lies with shifting scenes aloft:
Her brief kaleidoscopes of days, the shards
Of momentary anguish like a rift
Between her parts of self. She hears the words
She spoke in deepest anger, and the face
That felt the torture of her gaze. Sometimes
She's afraid to sleep or wake, the trace
Of dread on either side. Her mother gleams
In barefoot memories of an open door,
And she runs to a checkered apron gone
To absence. Childhood always ends up nowhere.
She longs for a trace to put her soul upon.
But there is nothing in the pilgrimages.
She sees smoke drift in subtle messages.

XII.

And when she sleeps there is forgetfulness,
And there in the great aisles of death she walks
Where she does not remember, like a trance
Of the nightgowns. And later when she speaks
Will the glints of passageway inform the sea
That washes in her brain? And when she rises
Will she choose a seashell battering memory
With its tympani of sound? And when it pleases
Will she think that this is heaven? Yes
And no. Meanwhile she turns the way she did
When she was a child, the embryo caress
In an envelope of sheets. Is that God's forehead
Creasing the sky? She thinks He whispers truth,
Then turns to see some children practice death.

XIII.

In the morning she wants coffee, strong enough
To make her feel alive. She's left the seed
Out for the birds; they fling each other off
To fill the speckled sequence of their need.
Perhaps she'll call her son today, and he'll
Tell her a story that will make her smile.
Perhaps she'll go out somewhere where she'll marvel
At the chance gathering of people, all
Of whom will decorate themselves for life.
There are people to play the music, to dance
To tambourines and drums, to mingle leaf
And flower, age and birth. There is one chance
At life. They fling off temporary cages
Like masters. They dramatize the passages.

XIV.

Meanwhile she wants to watch the children leave
For school, like leaves themselves flung out to change
The world with color. Never will they have
This way of life again, extraordinary range
Of hope. She looks for the lost leaf boys of the dark
And finds their faces glinting with the gold
That others bring. They get on the bus and shriek
To parents, trucks, dogs: theirs is the untold
Pleasure of being alive. In layers on
The day, the memory of her son in hat
And parka, leaning out the window, then
Her own face layered on the furthest seat,
Smiling. Childhood teases with its spurning
In ways that capture the hyperbolic yearning.

XV.

The leaves are falling; she will clean her yard.
The rake will harvest all the wrecked and robbed
Reminders of what's lost. It is absurd
To think of all their grace, now that she's stabbed
Their brilliance. Gathering them in piles, she wants
To burn them, have the splendor of the day
Distilled in the bonfires of her childhood haunts,
The danger spelled in a passionate bouquet
Of fireworks. But she thinks better of it,
Bags them up, and offers them curbside
For trash. It's just as well. The smell of rot
Strangely appeals to her, her own outside
Skin. How else to feel the subtle turning
Of the soul in the last felt moment of its burning?

About the Author

Kim Bridgford was born in 1959 and grew up in Coal Valley, Illinois. She received a B.A. in English and an M.F.A. in creative writing from the University of Iowa, and a Ph.D. in English from the University of Illinois. Her poetry has appeared in *North American Review, The Christian Science Monitor,* and *The Iowa Review,* her fiction in *The Georgia Review, The Massachusetts Review,* and *Redbook.* She lives with her husband, Pete Duval, and their son, Nick, in Connecticut, where she is a professor of English at Fairfield University and poetry editor of *Dogwood.* In 1994 she was named Connecticut Professor of the Year by the Carnegie Foundation for the Advancement of Teaching, and she was the recipient of a 1999 NEA Fellowship. Her letterpress book of poems, *Eden's Gift,* is forthcoming from Aralia Press.

Jo Yarrington is a professor in the Department of Visual
and Performing Arts, Fairfield University, Fairfield, CT. Her
sculptures, photographs, and installation pieces have been shown
in exhibitions at Artists Space and The Cathedral Church of
St. John the Divine in New York, Rotunda Gallery in Brooklyn,
the Aldrich Museum of Contemporary Art in Connecticut, the
DeCordova Museum and Sculpture Park in Massachusetts, I
Space Gallery in Chicago, Glasgow School of Art and Glasgow
University in Scotland, Galleria Sala Uno in Rome and Christus
Church in Cologne, Germany. She is a recipient of fellowships
from the Pollock Krasner Foundation, Pennsylvania Council on
the Arts, the Brandywine Institute, the Leighten Artists Colony
(Canada) and the MacDowell Colony.

Printed in the United States
1494700001B/112-135